Scrambler
and the Off-road Race

Illustrations by Pulsar

EGMONT

95% of the paper used in this book is recycled paper, the remaining 5% is an Egmont grade 5 paper that comes from well managed forests. For more information about Egmont's paper policy please visit www.egmont.co.uk/ethicalpublishing

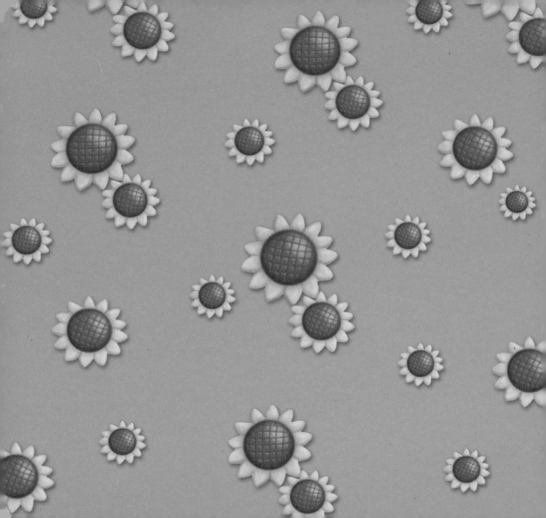

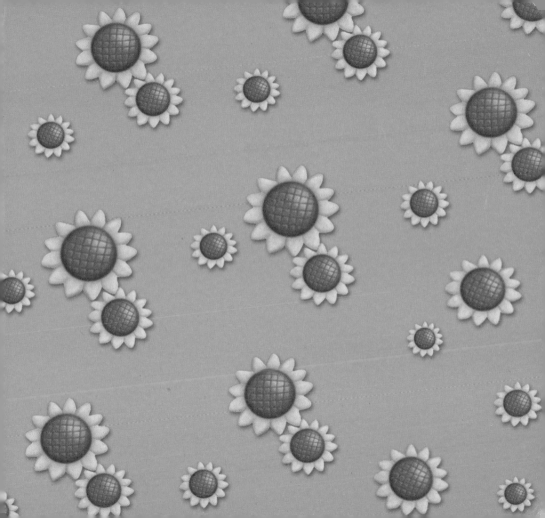

EGMONT
We bring stories to life

First published in Great Britain 2007
by Egmont UK Limited,
239 Kensington High Street, London W8 6SA

HiT entertainment

ISBN 978 1 4052 3144 2

1 3 5 7 9 10 8 6 4 2

Printed in Great Britain

Scrambler really wants to help Bob in Sunflower Valley. But how can an off-road racer be useful on a building site?

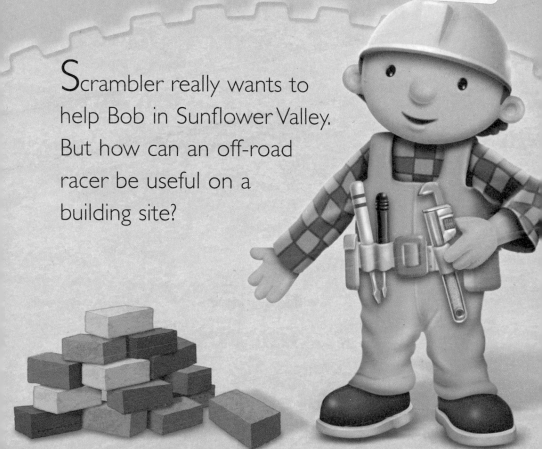

It was a lovely day in Sunflower Valley, and the team had a new job.

"We're building a barn for Farmer Pickles!" announced Bob.

Scruffty was excited. "Ruff! Ruff!" he barked, as he raced around Bob's legs.

But Bob didn't have time to play.

Scrambler was excited, too. He really wanted to help Bob and Wendy.

"What will I be doing?" he asked.

Bob shook his head.

"I'm sorry, Scrambler," he said.
"But there isn't really a job for you to do."

Scrambler was disappointed. But then Bob had an idea.

"There is something you can do," smiled Bob. "You can take Scruffty for a walk!"

"But that's not a proper job," said Scrambler, sadly.

"Yes it is," replied Bob. "You'll be keeping Scruffty safe."

The whole team was excited about building the barn.

"Can we build it?" Scoop asked.

"Yes we can!" the machines all cried.

"Er, yeah, I think so," added Lofty.

But poor Scrambler said nothing.
He trailed sadly off to walk Scruffty.

Scruffty ran on ahead, panting excitedly. "Ruff! Ruff!"

Scrambler followed slowly. He felt miserable.

"I can't believe I'm walking a dog!" he grumbled. "I thought I was going to get something important to do."

But when they got to the woods, Scrambler found he was starting to have fun with Scruffty. Especially when they played hide and seek!

When it was Scruffty's turn to hide, he ran off instead. The little dog didn't understand how to play the game!

Back at the site, everyone was working very hard.

Lofty was helping Bob and Wendy set up a wooden frame for the walls and roof of the barn.

Dizzy was pouring concrete to make the floor, and Roley was rolling it flat.

Scrambler and Scruffty chased each other until they found themselves in a beautiful valley, full of twisty paths and ditches.

"Wow!" exclaimed Scrambler. "Let's have an off-road race!"

"Ruff!" barked Scruffty, running ahead. The race was on!

The team had been busy all morning, and now the outside of the barn was completely finished.

"Excellent!" said Bob. "Now we need to build some shelves for Farmer Pickles to store things on."

"We'll need to concentrate," said Wendy. "It's a good thing Scruffty's not here!"

Scrambler and Scruffty were having the best time ever. They raced over rocks and through streams, getting very mucky.

"RUFF! RUFF! RUFF!" barked Scruffty, running through a hollow log.

"WHEEEEE!" cried Scrambler. "You can't catch me!"

At last, Scruffty landed in a big muddy puddle. Splash!

Back at the barn, work was finished. Bob and Wendy were having a rest and a cup of tea.

"I wonder where Scrambler's got to with Scruffty?" wondered Wendy, looking around.

Just then, Scrambler rumbled up. He was carrying something in his trailer.

"Scruffty's asleep!" said Scrambler.
"But I'm not tired." He tried not to yawn.

"See . . . dog-walking is a proper job,"
said Bob, lifting Scruffty from the trailer.
"And you made a friend!"

Scruffty woke up and licked his new
friend's nose. "Ruff!"

"Making friends is wicked!" Scrambler
grinned happily.

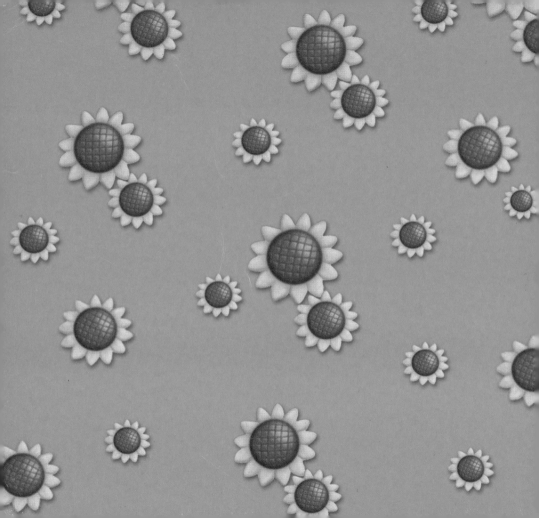

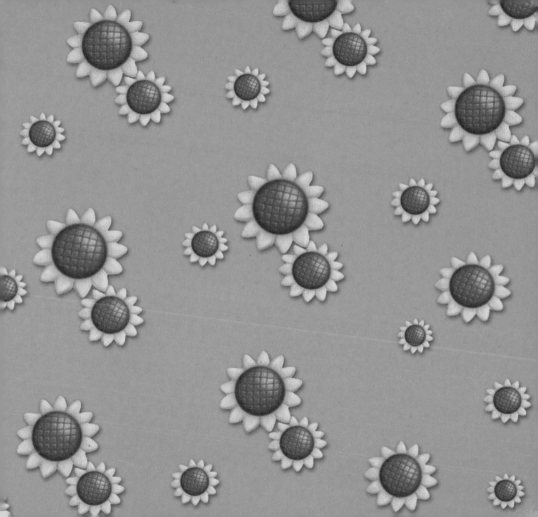

My Bob the Builder Story Library

ISBN: 978 1 4052 3142 8 • RRP: £2.99

ISBN: 978 1 4052 3143 5 • RRP: £2.99

ISBN: 978 1 4052 3144 2 • RRP: £2.99

ISBN: 978 1 4052 3140 4 • RRP: £2.99

My Bob the Builder Story Library is THE definitive collection of stories about Bob and the team. Start your Bob the Builder Story Library collection NOW and look out for even more titles to follow later!

Also available: My Bob the Builder Magnet Book
with 8 great magnets!

ISBN: 978 1 4052 3218 0   RRP: £5.99

A fantastic offer for Bob the Builder fans!

NOTE: Style of poster and door hanger may be different from those shown.

In every Bob the Builder Story Library book like this one, you will find a special token. Collect 4 tokens and we will send you a brilliant Bob the Builder poster and a double sided bedroom door hanger!

Simply tape a £1 coin in the space above and fill out the form overleaf.

To apply for this great offer, ask an adult to complete the details below and send this whole page with a £1 coin and 4 tokens, to:
BOB OFFERS, PO BOX 715, HORSHAM RH12 5WG

☐ Please send me a Bob the Builder poster and door hanger. I enclose 4 tokens plus a £1 coin (price includes P&P).

Fan's name: ....

Address: ....

....

Postcode: .... Email: ....

Date of birth: ....

Name of parent / guardian: ....

Signature of parent / guardian: ....

Please allow 28 days for delivery. Offer is only available while stocks last. We reserve the right to change the terms of this offer at any time and we offer a 14 day money back guarantee. This does not affect your statutory rights. Offers apply to UK only.

☐ We may occasionally wish to send you information about other Egmont children's books, including the next titles in the Bob the Builder Story Library series. If you would rather we didn't, please tick this box.

Ref: BOB 001